HORSE HOOVES
AND CHICKEN FEET

HORSE HOOVES AND CHICKEN FEET

MEXICAN FOLKTALES

SELECTED BY NEIL PHILIP

ILLUSTRATED BY
JACQUELINE MAIR

CLARION BOOKS

NEW YORK

WITH LOVE TO FRANCES D'SOUZA

—NP

WITH LOVE TO LOUISE, CHRIS, TOBY, AND JESSIE
FOR HELPING MY MEXICAN DREAM COME TRUE

—JM

Clarion Books

a Houghton Mifflin Company imprint

215 Park Avenue South, New York, NY 10003

Published in the United States in 2003 by arrangement with

The Albion Press Ltd, Spring Hill, Idbury, Oxfordshire OX7 6RU, England

Illustrations copyright © 2003 by Jacqueline Mair

Selection, introduction, notes, and retellings copyright © 2003 by Neil Philip

The author and publisher would like to thank the following copyright holders for permission to reprint
and retell the stories listed below. Every effort has been made to contact copyright holders, but we
would be interested to hear from any copyright holders not here acknowledged.
 University of California Press for "The Mule Drivers Who Lost Their Feet," from Stanley L. Robe,
Mexican Tales and Legends from Los Altos, copyright © 1970 by the Regents of the University of
California. The University of Chicago Press for "The Tailor Who Sold His Soul to the Devil," "Horse
Hooves and Chicken Feet," and "The Priest Who Had a Glimpse of Glory," from Américo Paredes,
Folktales of Mexico, copyright © 1970 by the University of Chicago.

Designed by Emma Bradford.

The illustrations were executed in acrylic on paper.
The text was set in 13-point ITC Garamond Book.

For information about permission to reproduce selections from this book,
write to Permissions, Houghton Mifflin Company, 215 Park Avenue South,
New York, NY 10003

www.houghtonmifflinbooks.com

Library of Congress Cataloging-in-Publication Data

Horse hooves and chicken feet : Mexican folktales / edited by
Neil Philip; illustrated by Jacqueline Mair. p. cm.
Includes bibliographical references.
ISBN 0-618-19463-0 (alk. paper)
1. Mexican Americans–Folklore. 2. Tales–Southwest, New. 3. Tales–Mexico.
[1. Mexican Americans–Folklore. 2. Folklore–Southwest, New. 3. Folklore–Mexico.]
I. Philip, Neil. II. Mair, Jacqueline, ill.
PZ8.1.H8616 2003
398 .2–dc21   2002154886

10 9 8 7 6 5 4 3 2 1

Typesetting: Servis Filmsetting Ltd, Manchester
Color origination: Classicscan, Singapore
Printed in China by Midas Printing International Ltd.

CONTENTS

INTRODUCTION

The desire to tell stories is one of the defining characteristics of humankind. From the dawn of time we have been telling ourselves tales: tales to make us laugh, tales to make us cry, tales to make us shiver, and, most of all, tales to make us wonder.

Just as each individual has his or her unique storytelling style, so each culture has its own folktale tradition. These traditions are an intrinsic part of their respective cultures, and are remarkably robust. It might be thought that the immense popularity over the past two hundred years of the German folktales collected by the Brothers Grimm had created a kind of uniform global folk literature by now. But it has not. The reason for this is that the authority of a folktale does not rest in written versions but in the living words of oral storytellers. The tales pass from mouth to mouth, and from this they derive both their vitality and their individuality.

Although the plots—what folklorists call the "tale types"—of some of the Mexican folktales in this book can be found in the Grimms' collection, the atmosphere and flavor of these tales is completely different. The Mexican and Mexican American tradition is, for instance, suffused with religious imagery drawn from Roman Catholicism to an unparalleled degree. Yet the religious element in the tales does not make them somber or difficult—instead, it makes them sparkle with life and meaning.

In the story "The Two Marias" (which is related to "Cinderella") the role of the fairy godmother is taken by the Virgin Mary. In both

1

INTRODUCTION

"The Shadow" and "Cinder Juan," the soul of a dead man can be admitted to heaven only after a performing a good deed. In "The Priest Who Had a Glimpse of Glory," centuries elapse during a moment's contemplation of the wonders of paradise.

Mexican tales invite us into a magical world of enchantment and transformation—but also into a world of reality, of love and loss and sudden reversals of fortune. Like the popular Mexican folk character Pedro the Trickster, positioned at the very entrance to heaven, the Mexican storyteller is perfectly placed to observe the comings and goings of the good and the bad, and is equally amused by both of them.

Some of the stories in this book were collected in Mexico proper, and many others from the Mexican population of Colorado and New Mexico. The stories themselves are largely of continental Spanish origin; and like Spanish stories, they also show some influence from that great treasure house *The Arabian Nights* (which may be traced back to the centuries of Moorish rule over Spain). Like plants, the stories have naturalized in their new habitat, so that they now have a unique flavor of their own. This is a matter not just of what one might call the stage sets and props of the stories, but of their viewpoint. Like Pedro the Trickster, they see life as both profoundly serious and essentially comic.

An example is "The Cat and the Mouse," included by John O. West in his excellent survey *Mexican-American Folklore*. It is a funny story with a serious sting in its tail.

> A cat was chasing a mouse, but the mouse made it safely back into its hole.
>
> The cat sat patiently outside, trying to coax the mouse out.
>
> *"Meow, meow,"* it whispered. But the mouse was no fool, and it stayed inside.
>
> So the cat barked, *"Bow, wow!"*

INTRODUCTION

> The mouse, thinking the coast must be clear, came
> out—and the cat ate him up.
>   As the cat was cleaning his whiskers, he said, "It's
> so useful to speak two languages."

Mexican stories revel in both cleverness and stupidity—as much in the tale of the numskulls in "The Mule Drivers Who Lost Their Feet" as in the tale of the quick-witted protagonist in "The Tailor Who Sold His Soul to the Devil."

The sheer magic of the Mexican story world can be felt in longer tales, such as "The Story of the Sun and the Moon" and "The Brave Widow." It is a magic that is rooted in a sense of rightness and a sense of wonder. In "The Green Bird," a New Mexican story collected by José Manuel Espinosa but not included in this book, the heroine saves her true love from a witch's enchantment. As they flee from the witch, they transform themselves successively into a palm tree and a coyote, a church and a sacristan, and a shepherd with a sheepdog. They change their shapes simply by deciding to do so. It is this matter-of-fact faith in the transforming power of the imagination that lies at the heart of Mexican storytelling.

Folklorists such as José Manuel Espinosa, Juan B. Rael, and Stanley L. Robe have gathered a rich haul of stories from the lips of storytellers in Mexico and the Hispanic Southwest. These marvelous stories are not as widely known as they should be, perhaps because the collectors generally published them in colloquial Spanish and did not translate them into English.

The storytellers whose narratives were collected by folklorists such as Espinosa and Rael were not professionals. They were, as Rael puts it, "mostly farmers, stock raisers, farm laborers, sheepherders, housewives, and the inhabitants of small communities engaged in miscellaneous occupations." Nevertheless, many of them were consummate verbal artists whose work deserves to be

3

read unmediated in the original Spanish. I realized only when writing the Notes on the Stories that I had chosen from J. M. Espinosa's haul of 114 tales no fewer than three from the same talented narrator, Benigna Vigil: "The Shadow," "The Two Marias," and "The Seven Oxen."

In his book *Amapa Storytellers,* the folklorist Stanley L. Robe records the childhood memories of one such storyteller, Salvador González Quesada, in a way that shows both how such tales are transmitted and why they survive. As a child, González attended nightly tale sessions at the home of storyteller Sabino López:

> At nightfall the children used to say: *"Vamos con don Sabino"* ("Let's go to don Sabino's house"). There he gathered the children around him in a circle and they listened to him. Outside there were petroleum lamps at the street corners. These flickery affairs gave very poor light but enough to permit one to see his way home along the cobblestone streets of the village. Early in the evening each lamp was filled with a half-liter of oil and when it was gone, the light went out. The children inside don Sabino's house always kept one eye on the storyteller and the other on the lamp out on the street corner, hoping that they might squeeze in one more story before the light went out and they could still see their way home.

I offer these retellings in a spirit of tribute to such storytellers, in the hope that this book may help keep the lamp alight.

NEIL PHILIP

THE FLEA

Once there was a man who was a great magician. His daughter fell in love with a boy, and the magician said, "I will let you marry him if he can outsmart me."

He told the boy, "If, over the next three nights, you can sleep where my spells cannot find you, then you may marry my daughter."

Now, the boy was a magician, too—though the father did not know this. So the boy thought hard, and on the first night he rocked himself to sleep on the horns of the moon.

Next day when the boy turned up, the magician said, "It can't be very comfortable sleeping on the moon."

The boy was amazed. Now, where should he sleep tonight?

On the second night he slept snug inside a shell in the depths of the sea. But the magician cast his spells and found him there.

When the boy came to see him in the morning, he said, "You must be very fond of salt, to sleep at the bottom of the sea."

Gracious! Where could he sleep tonight where the magician would not find him?

He went out the door, turned himself into a flea, and hopped onto the door jamb. Then, when the magician went outside to cast his spells, the enchanted flea jumped onto the rim of his sombrero.

The magician could not find the boy anywhere. He looked up. He looked down. He looked all around. But there was no sign of him. He couldn't understand it.

THE FLEA

At last he gave up and went home—with the flea still perched on his hat. When he went through the door, the flea hopped back onto the door jamb and settled down for a good night's sleep.

The next morning when the boy came to wish him good day, the magician could not tell him where he had slept.

"You have outwitted me," he said, "and won my daughter's hand."

So the boy married the magician's daughter, and on the first night they slept on the horns of the moon, on the second they slept at the bottom of the sea, and on the third they turned themselves into fleas and slept on the rim of her father's sombrero.

THE STORY OF THE SUN AND THE MOON

Once there was a soldier who woke up one night and thought for a moment that a girl was standing in the doorway of his room. He rubbed his eyes, but when he looked again, she was gone. *I must have been dreaming,* he thought.

Next night he decided to stay awake and keep watch, just in case. The way the moonlight and shadow fell, it was hard to see clearly, but at midnight he was sure he could see her again. He lit a candle so he could be certain. But as soon as he had done so, he received a violent blow in the face, as if the air itself had hit him. He dropped the candle, and the hot wax spilled over the floor. The girl seemed to vanish into thin air.

But the soldier had seen enough. The girl was as beautiful as starlight, and he had fallen head-over-heels in love.

"I will go and search for her," he said.

He set out at first light. Some way along the road he came across two men who were fighting furiously—they were rolling in the dust and hitting each other.

"What's your quarrel?" asked the soldier.

"We are brothers," they replied, "and we are fighting over our inheritance."

"That is no reason to fight," said the soldier. "Can't you agree?"

"No!" said the men. And then each of them shouted, "They're mine!" and they began fighting again.

"Stop! Stop!" said the soldier. "Tell me the problem, and I will solve it for you. I don't know you, so I will treat you both the same."

"That makes sense," said one brother.

"It does," agreed the other.

"Our father had three great treasures," said the first. "These magic boots, which carry the wearer three leagues with every step; this magic cudgel, which brings the dead back to life; and this magic hat, which makes the person who wears it invisible to witches."

"And they should all be mine!" said the second brother. "I was Papa's favorite!"

"No!" said the first brother. "They should all be mine! I am the eldest."

"You both have a point," said the soldier. "This is a hard case. But I do have a solution. When I say 'Go!' you must both run to that hill over there. Leave the treasures with me. The first one to get back will be the winner."

The brothers agreed.

"Go!" shouted the soldier, and away they ran like a pair of coyotes.

When they got back, still neck and neck, the soldier was gone, and so were the treasures.

"Well," said the eldest, "he did say he would solve our problem."

"So he did," agreed his brother. And, all told, so long as the other one did not have the treasures, they were both content.

Now that he had the magic boots, the soldier covered the ground with astonishing speed, advancing three leagues with every step. Soon he had gone so far that he arrived at the house of the Sun.

He knocked at the door, and an old woman answered.

"Good evening, grandmother," said the soldier.

"What are you doing here, young man?" she asked.

"I am looking for the beautiful girl who appeared in my room and then disappeared again," he said. "Did she pass this way?"

"Yes," said the old woman, "but she is long gone now. And so should you be. If you are still here when my son comes home, he will eat you up!"

Just then they heard the sound of the Sun approaching.

When the Sun saw the soldier, he shouted, "Mama! Mama! There is a human being! Give him to me! I will eat him!"

But the old woman replied, "No, my son. It is only a poor traveler who is stopping here. Leave him be!" And then she gave the Sun a box on the ear.

So the soldier traveled on, three leagues at every step, until he came to the house of the Moon. He knocked at the door, and it was opened by an old woman.

"Good evening, grandmother," he said.

"What are you doing here, young man?" she asked him, and he told her all about the girl he was looking for.

"She is long gone," said the old woman, "and so should you be. If my son finds you here, he will eat you up."

Just then the Moon came home. When he saw the soldier, he squealed with delight. "A human being!" he said. "Give him to me, and I will eat him!"

But the old woman replied, "No, my son. It is only a poor traveler who is stopping here. Leave him be!" And she boxed both the Moon's ears.

The soldier traveled on, three leagues at every step, until he came to the house of the Wind.

He knocked at the door, and it was opened by the Wind himself. The Wind was weeping great hot tears like raindrops.

"What is the matter?" asked the soldier.

"My mother has just died," said the Wind. And inside the house the soldier saw the body of an old woman.

"I can help," he said. He took out the magic cudgel and hit the old woman with it three times.

She got up, unsteady as a newborn foal, and said, "Son! Where have I been?"

The Wind did not reply. Instead, he asked the soldier, "How can I ever repay you?

The soldier said, "Help me find my true love. She is a beautiful maiden who appeared and then disappeared, and I have tracked her past the house of the Sun and past the house of the Moon."

"I will come with you," said the Wind, "and help if I can."

They set off, but the soldier kept having to stop to let the Wind catch up.

"Lend me one of those magic boots," said the Wind. "Then we will be able to talk as we go."

The soldier did so, and finally they arrived at a witch's house.

"This is the place," said the Wind. "You will be safe from the witch in your magic hat. Go in." And then the Wind took leave of the soldier and went back to his mother.

The soldier found the witch warming herself by the fire. There was a young woman there, too, but she was not the girl the soldier was looking for.

At last the girl said, "Can I take some food to my sister?"

But the witch replied, "No! Let her starve! That will teach her to fall in love with a no-good soldier!"

When the soldier heard that, he knew that the girl must be somewhere nearby. He went through the entire house looking for her. He opened seven doors with seven locks, and behind the last one he found her.

This girl was not a witch, so she could see him.

"You have come!" she said.

"Yes," he said. "I have come." And they embraced.

Then the soldier took out his knife and cut the magic hat in two and gave one half to the maiden. He took off his magic boot and cut that in two and gave one half to the maiden. And lastly he cut the magic cudgel in two and gave one half to the maiden. "From now on we shall share everything," he said.

"Now let us make our escape," she replied.

THE STORY OF THE SUN AND THE MOON

They fled from the house, one and a half leagues with every step, but it was not fast enough. Soon they heard the old witch hard on their heels. With only half the hat each, they were not completely invisible, and the witch could track them by their shadows.

The maiden took a comb from her hair and threw it behind her. Where it fell, a forest of spiny pine trees grew up in the witch's path, while the soldier and the maiden fled.

But it was not long before they heard the old witch once more.

This time the maiden reached into her pocket and took out a thimbleful of ashes and scattered them behind her, where they turned into a thick fog in the witch's path, while the soldier and the maiden fled.

But it was not long before they heard the old witch once more.

This time the maiden flung down a thimbleful of salt. It turned into a great river behind them, which the old witch could not cross.

Then the old woman sat down on the bank and began to weep, crying, "Oh, ungrateful daughter! May your dreams run dry at the wellspring!"

The maiden turned to the soldier and said, "Remember, you have released me from my mother's house but not from my mother's curse."

When they came near to the soldier's home, they arrived at a spring of water. The soldier said to the maiden, "You wait here. I will go to my parents' house and tell them the good news."

"Very well," said the maiden. "But first let me tie my handkerchief to your belt, so that you will not forget me. And remember, do not allow your parents, or your brother, or your sister, or any of your family, to embrace you before you have come back to the spring to fetch me."

"I will not," said the soldier.

But as soon as he arrived home, his grandmother threw her arms

around him, and he instantly forgot all about the beautiful maiden who was waiting for him at the spring of water.

The parents of the soldier were overjoyed to have him home.

"Now he has done his wandering," said his mother. "It is time for him to marry and settle down."

So they found a girl for him to marry, and arranged the wedding for the very next day.

Waiting and waiting at the wellspring, the maiden realized that the soldier was never coming back for her. "He has forgotten me," she said. "My dreams have run dry."

She walked sadly into town, where she found the soldier about to be married to the girl his parents had found for him.

She begged to be allowed to entertain the wedding party.

When everyone was there, she clapped her hands together, and a pair of doves flew out.

The maiden reached out her arms to the male dove and called, "Do you remember, ungrateful little dove, how you released me from my mother's house but not from my mother's curse?"

"Kurukuku," cooed the dove. "I do not remember."

She reached out her arms again and called, "Do you remember, ungrateful little dove, that you left me at the spring of water?"

"Kurukuku," cooed the dove. "I am beginning to remember."

She reached out her arms again and called, "Do you remember, ungrateful little dove, that I tied my handkerchief to your belt?"

"Kurukuku," cooed the dove. "I remember! I remember!"

And the soldier looked down and saw the handkerchief tied to his belt, and he remembered everything.

He turned to his bride-to-be and told her, "I am sorry. I cannot marry you. I am promised to another."

Then the soldier embraced the maiden, and they were married right then and there. And the Sun shone brightly on their days, the Moon shone softly on their nights, and the Wind blew gently at their backs, all the years of their lives.

THE TAILOR WHO SOLD HIS SOUL TO THE DEVIL

Once there was a tailor who had no money to feed his family. He didn't know where to turn.

"I'd even accept help from the Devil," he said.

As soon as the words were out of his mouth, the Devil appeared. "I will help you," the Devil said, "if I can have your soul in return."

The tailor thought about it. "All right," he said. "You can have my soul . . . so long as you can beat me in a sewing contest."

"It's a deal!" said the Devil. He rubbed his hands together with delight at the thought of winning another soul.

The Devil gave the tailor a sack of gold, enough to feed his family for seven years, and then the two of them sat down with two piles of cloth to turn into shirts.

The Devil had trouble threading his needle, and the tailor said, "Let me do that for you."

He threaded the Devil's needle with the longest thread he could find. When they began to sew, the Devil's thread kept getting caught up in itself, and he had to stop constantly to untangle it.

Meanwhile, the tailor threaded his own needle with a very short thread, with which he sewed so fast that it took the Devil's breath away.

So the tailor finished first, and the Devil never got his soul.

And that is why, when daughters thread their needles with a long thread, their mothers say, "Girl, that is the Devil's thread!"

THE HOG

Once there was a man who had a fattened hog that was ready for butchering. Whenever one of his neighbors killed a hog, they always shared the meat. But now that it was his turn, this man wanted to keep it all for himself. "Why should they have any?" he said to his only friend. "I fed it. I raised it. It should all be mine."

His friend said, "Let's kill the hog tonight and hide the meat. In the morning we can tell anyone who asks that the hog has been stolen."

"Why didn't I think of that!" said the man.

So in secret, in the dead of night, the two men butchered the hog. The next morning the owner of the hog went to slice some bacon for his breakfast, but he couldn't find the meat anywhere. That's because his friend had gotten up early and stolen it all.

The man decided to go from house to house asking if anyone had seen his hog. The first house was that of his friend.

"Compadre!" he said. "My hog has been stolen!"

"Excellent! Very convincing!" said the friend. "If you tell everyone else just like that, they're sure to believe you."

"No," said the man, "it really *is* missing. I've been robbed!"

"Oh, so that's your game," said the friend. "If you are so ungrateful that you won't even share it with me after all I've done for you, may God help you."

So the friend got the whole hog, and the man was left with nothing—and some say he was too mean to share even that with his neighbors.

PEDRO THE TRICKSTER

There was a man who had an only son, named Pedro. Pedro grew up with a good heart but wild ways. He was always gambling and getting into trouble. But whenever he got into trouble, he always got out of it again, so he earned the nickname Pedro de Ordimalas, or Pedro the Trickster.

When Pedro was old enough, he got married. He loved his wife and was good to her in his way, but they were always poor, because Pedro gambled away any money he got. And if he didn't gamble it away, like as not he gave it away.

One day Pedro was gambling in a cantina. He had run right out of money—he had lost it all. There was a knocking at the door, and it was two poor old beggars. Pedro didn't know it, but it was the Lord and Saint Peter, come to see who was generous and who was not.

Pedro's heart was touched, and he asked his friends to lend him fifty centavos. "No," they said. "You'll only waste it by giving it to those worthless beggars." But Pedro told them he would not.

"I'm coming right back," he said, "and then you can win it back again."

So his friends lent Pedro the fifty centavos, and he rushed out and overtook the beggars and gave them the money.

The Lord said, "Thank you, Pedro. As you have given me a gift, I will give one to you. Name your reward."

And Pedro replied, "I would like my fifty centavos back, please, so I can return to my friends and show them that I still have it."

"That is not enough," said the Lord. "Ask for a real reward."

"I would like it if, when I go somewhere and I don't want to leave, no one could make me leave, not even God the Father Himself."

"Ask for more," said the Lord.

"I would like a deck of cards that always wins," said Pedro.

"Ask for more," said the Lord.

"I would like a drum that will not stop beating unless I say so."

"Ask for more," said the Lord.

And now Pedro realized to whom he was speaking. "I would like You to take my father and my mother and all my brothers and sisters and my wife and my children, when the time comes," he said.

"And do you want anything for yourself?" asked the Lord.

"That when You take me, You take my body as well as my soul, so that I shall never die," said Pedro.

"Your wish shall be granted," said the Lord.

Pedro went back to the cantina and started gambling with the fifty centavos that the Lord had given back to him. And he found that whereas before he had always lost, now he always won. He spent all his time in the cantina, gambling and winning with the pack of cards that the Lord had given him.

When news came that all of his family had fallen sick and died, Pedro was very sad, but he told himself, "At least the Lord has taken them, and they are now in heaven."

Pedro kept winning, and soon he was very rich. "What shall I do with all this money?" he asked himself.

One night he was sitting at home, warming himself by the fire, when he heard a knock at the door. It was the Death who rides a white horse. Death said, "I have been sent by the Lord Jesus Christ to fetch you."

Pedro said, "All right. But first can I ask you to beat this drum, to call all the poor people here, so that I can divide my wealth among them?"

"It will be a pleasure," said Death.

And Death began to beat on the drum—and soon found that she could not stop.

Pedro just left her there and went off to the cantina as usual. He didn't return home for a week, and when he did, found Death there, still beating the drum.

"Pedro, what are you going to do with me?" asked Death. "The Lord is waiting for me. He has other Deaths to send about his business, but, still, he will be worried about me. Please let me go."

"Very well," said Pedro, "I will let you go so long as you pardon me all the years I have lived so far and give me as many years again as I have already had."

"Your wish shall be granted," said Death.

The Death who rides a white horse went back to the Lord and told Him it was impossible to fetch Pedro.

After Pedro had lived the extra years he had won from Death, the Lord sent the Death who carries a scythe to fetch him. But the same thing happened as before, and Pedro won yet more years by tricking Death with his drum.

When the time came round again, the Lord sent the Death who drives a cart, with strict instructions to fetch Pedro no matter what tricks he got up to.

It was noon, and Pedro was fixing his midday meal when he heard the creaking of Death's cart outside his door.

"So you have come at last, friend Death," he said.

"Yes," she replied. And then she said, "Just close your eyes for a moment."

Pedro closed his eyes, and Death carried him off in an instant.

Now, the Lord had to decide what to do with Pedro. He decided to send him to look after the children in Limbo. But after a day or two the children went to Saint Peter and complained about Pedro. "He keeps trying to drown us," they said.

Saint Peter asked Pedro what he thought he was doing,

drowning the children he had been sent to look after. "I was not drowning them," Pedro said. "I was baptizing them in the river."

Saint Peter said, "Since you cannot behave yourself in Limbo, I shall send you to Purgatory."

Once there, Pedro took pity on all the poor souls who were living there. "I can help you to end your penance more quickly," he said.

"No, thank you," they replied. "We will leave the years of our penance to the Lord."

But Pedro would not take no for an answer. He made himself a long whip and began to beat the souls in Purgatory, to hasten the end of their trials.

The souls went to Saint Peter and complained about Pedro. "He is unbearable," they said.

Saint Peter took their complaint to the Lord, and the Lord said, "There is nothing else for it. We must send Pedro to Hell."

In Hell, Pedro was put to work fetching and carrying for the devils. They decided to hold a fiesta, and they asked Pedro to arrange the table and serve the meal. Pedro set everything out beautifully, but he painted all the chairs with sticky black pitch.

At the end of the meal, the devils said, "Pedro, clear the table."

"Not until I have given thanks to God for the meal," he said. "That is what I have always done."

"Well, don't do it here," said the devils.

But Pedro did not listen to them. "Thanks be to God," he said, "and hail, Holy Mary."

The devils nearly jumped out of their chairs with fright when they heard the holy names, but they could not, because they were stuck fast. They kept jumping up and down with the chairs stuck to their backsides, bumping into each other. Pedro had locked the doors, so the devils were fighting each other to get out the windows. Meanwhile Pedro kept shouting louder and louder, "Hail, Holy Mary!"

PEDRO THE TRICKSTER

The devils went to Saint Peter to complain about Pedro. "He will drive us mad with his bless this and bless that," they said.

Saint Peter went to the Lord and told Him that not even the devils could put up with Pedro.

"Find him a flock of sheep to look after," said the Lord. "He can't get into any trouble tending sheep."

Saint Peter sent Pedro to a grassy meadow filled with wildflowers and gave him a flock of sheep to look after. In the distance Pedro could see a beautiful mansion, and he drove his sheep toward it.

When he got there, Pedro found Saint Peter standing outside the door, with a great golden key in his hand.

"What is this house?" asked Pedro.

"This is the Mansion of Glory," said Saint Peter.

"Can I have a glimpse inside?" asked Pedro.

"Just one glimpse," said Saint Peter, and he opened the door a crack.

As soon as Saint Peter opened the door, Pedro stepped onto the threshold.

Saint Peter grabbed hold of him. "Come out of the doorway," he said. But Pedro would not come out.

Saint Peter called the Lord, and the Lord told Pedro to come out. But Pedro said, "Was it not You who told me that not even God the Father could make me come out of somewhere if I did not want to?"

So the Lord said, "Very well. But you may not enter heaven. I will turn you to stone right here in the entrance."

"Yes, Lord," said Pedro. "That will suit me very well. So long as I keep my eyes, so that I can see everything that happens here."

And there Pedro remains, at the entrance to paradise, where he can keep watch on the comings and goings of saints and sinners alike.

THE SHADOW

There was once a poor married couple who had no children. They begged God for a baby, and at last He granted their wish and gave them a son. They asked some rich people from another city to be the baby's godparents. Since the parents were so poor, the priest said that the godparents should be the ones to educate little Juanito.

So when the boy was old enough, his godparents took charge of him to educate him. And when they had finished, they sent him back to his parents, who were no longer poor but had become quite wealthy by buying things cheap and selling them high.

The young man was so well educated that his parents didn't know what to do with him. So they sent him out into the world to trade. They gave him three mules loaded with money and told him to buy things in other lands. "Be sure to make this money work for you," they said. "Remember, the golden rule is: Buy cheap, sell high."

The young man set out. After he had gone a long way, he sat down to rest, but his rest was disturbed by the sound of wailing from a house by the road. He went to investigate and found a woman weeping over the body of her husband. She had been crying for three days. She told him that she could not afford to bury her husband, and that the men to whom he had owed money were calling in the debts. She didn't know what to do.

The young man felt so sorry for her that he led his mules over, unloaded all the money, and gave it to the widow so that she could bury her husband and pay off his debts. They called for the priest and buried the man, and then the woman paid off all the creditors so they would leave her in peace.

The young man turned around and went home. When his parents saw him, they said, "Here comes Don Juanito."

He told them what had happened on the way. They were not at all pleased. They said, "What kind of education is this? The boy doesn't have the sense he was born with!" Nevertheless they sent him out again, with three mules loaded with money, to buy things in other countries. "Remember," they called after him, "buy cheap, sell high."

He came to a kingdom by the sea and announced that he would buy whatever was for sale.

There was a man who had three princesses. He had kidnapped them and didn't know what to do with them. So he offered them to Don Juanito.

Don Juanito felt sorry for the princesses. He asked the man if he would accept a mule-load of money in exchange for the three girls, but the man said, "Only *one* mule-load for three princesses? That would be like giving them away!"

The princesses were crying and begging Don Juanito to ransom them. The young man's heart melted, and he said, "Would you accept two mule-loads?"

"You drive a hard bargain," said the man. "But as I like your face, I'll let you have them for three mule-loads, though I'm selling them at a loss."

So Don Juanito paid the man all three mule-loads of money to free the princesses.

Then Don Juanito set out for home with the three girls. When his parents saw him coming, they said, "Here comes Don Juanito, bringing home the goods he has bought. This time everything must have gone well."

When he got there, they said, "Tell us the good news."

"I've brought you three princesses to keep you company," he said. "Now you will never be lonely."

They were even less pleased than before. "What kind of education is this? The boy's a complete fool!" they said. "Instead of profit, you have brought us more expense. Well, you needn't think that we will look after these girls for you. We will give you an allowance of four *reales* a day, and you and your girls can live on that."

Don Juanito looked after the girls as if he were their father. At night, the three princesses slept on the mattress and Don Juanito slept at their feet, with his head pillowed on the youngest girl's ankles.

One day the eldest princess said to him, "Why don't you scavenge some rags from the trash and bring them to me?"

He did as she suggested, and from the rags she stitched beautiful good-luck charms for him to sell at rich people's houses. He sold them all and came home with his pockets full of money.

"Now we don't want you to work anymore," said the princess. She told him to go to the plaza and buy her rags of every color, to make more charms. He did that, and to one of the charms the princess attached a letter to her parents, the king and queen, and told Don Juanito to give it to a sailor.

Don Juanito went down to the harbor and gave the bag to a sailor whose ship was just setting sail.

Out at sea the sailor could not resist reading the letter. When he realized that the three princesses were alive and well, he was so pleased that he decorated his ship with red flags and sailed home as fast as he could.

When the king and queen saw the ship all decked out with red flags, the queen said, "My heart is beating so fast! Perhaps our daughters are coming home!"

"Or their bones," said the king.

When the ship sailed into port, the king hailed it. "What news?" he shouted. "We're half dead with anxiety."

The sailor showed him the letter.

"Our daughters are alive!" shouted the king, and the queen fainted.

The letter told the king where the princesses were and who had freed them from captivity.

The sailor offered to sail straight back to fetch the princesses home. "Be as quick as you can," said the king. On board the ship was a beautiful carriage for the three princesses.

The sailor arrived at Don Juanito's house and said the king had sent him to fetch Don Juanito and the princesses. Don Juanito asked his parents if he could go, and they said yes, so he climbed into the sailor's carriage with the princesses, and off they went.

They boarded the ship and sailed away.

Out at sea the sailor fell in love with the youngest princess, who was the one who loved Don Juanito. The sailor noticed that Don Juanito always rested his head on her ankles while they slept, and became jealous. So on the second night at sea the sailor woke him, saying, "Don Juanito! Come out on deck and see how beautiful the stars are tonight."

While Don Juanito was gazing at the stars, the sailor pushed him over the side, and he plunged into the sea.

Don Juanito could not swim, and he thought that he would drown. But it seemed to him that a shadowy figure came and rescued him and carried him safely to an island in the middle of the sea. Or perhaps it was just a piece of driftwood he was holding on to.

When the princesses woke and found Don Juanito missing, they could not understand what had happened. "Perhaps he fell overboard," the sailor told them. They cried and cried for the loss of Don Juanito.

When they arrived at the palace, they told their parents everything. It should have been such a happy homecoming, but all the girls were weeping and nothing would console them.

THE SHADOW

The king and queen were overjoyed to have their daughters back but very sad that the one who had rescued them had disappeared.

Meanwhile, Don Juanito had found fresh water on the island, and he lived there as best he could on wild herbs and berries. After seven years his clothes had rotted away, and with his long, matted hair and shaggy beard he looked like a wild animal.

By this time the two older princesses were married, but Don Juanito's sweetheart had no wish to marry anyone. The king and queen wanted her to marry the sailor, but she refused. Finally, the king grew angry and told her she must marry the sailor whether she liked it or not. They began to plan the wedding. But the youngest daughter's only preparation was a cup of poison, to be drunk the night before the ceremony.

On the night before the wedding Don Juanito heard a voice, whispering, "Don Juanito, Don Juanito, your sweetheart is getting married." It was the shadow who had saved his life seven years before.

"God bless her and make her happy," said Don Juanito.

And then the shadow said, "If you promise to pay me half of what God gives you in the first three years of your marriage, I will take you to her."

"I promise," said Don Juanito.

"Close your eyes and don't open them until I set you down," the shadow said. "Now, climb onto my back."

Don Juanito climbed onto the shadow's back, and they rose into the air. The shadow carried him across the ocean and set him down outside the palace of the king.

The shadow told Don Juanito, "You can open your eyes." But when he opened them, no one was there.

Don Juanito went to the castle gates and begged to see the king. The guards wanted to turn him away because he looked like a wild man, but the king came out and asked him who he was and what he wanted.

32

"My name is Don Juanito," he said, "and I want to marry my true love, the youngest princess."

The king could hardly believe that this naked, filthy creature all covered in hair was the handsome Don Juanito, but he took him to a room where servants washed him and cut his hair and dressed him in fine clothes. Then he sat him on a throne and called his eldest daughter in.

"Don Juanito!" she shouted.

Then he called his second daughter in.

"Don Juanito!" she shouted. "Don Juanito!"

So then the king knew that the man really was the lost Don Juanito. He sent the servants to fetch his youngest daughter.

When they came to her room, she had just raised the cup of poison to her lips. "What is it?" she asked.

"Your father wants you," the servants said. So the youngest princess set down the cup of poison and went to see her father.

When she entered the room and saw Don Juanito sitting on the throne, she flung herself at his feet, crying, "Don Juanito! Don Juanito! Don Juanito! My true love!"

Then the king sent for the sailor. When he saw Don Juanito, he began to tremble and shake. Don Juanito told the king how the sailor had thrown him into the sea. The king ordered that the sailor be tied to a wild mule and dragged behind it until every bone in his body had been broken.

The youngest princess and Don Juanito were married with great celebrations. They lived happily together for three years, and at the end of that time God blessed them with a beautiful baby boy.

That same night Don Juanito heard a whisper in his ear.

"I have come for what was promised," the shadow said.

"Half of all my wealth," said Don Juanito.

"Half of *everything* God has given you," said the shadow, looking at the baby.

THE SHADOW

Poor Don Juanito felt as if the sky had fallen on his head. "You bought my promise cheap and now are selling it high," he said.

But he could not break his word.

Don Juanito took his baby son from the cradle and raised his sword to cut him in two.

When the shadow saw that Don Juanito was going to keep his promise, he said, "Stop! Don't do it! Everything is yours. I am the man whose burial you paid for. This was the good deed I needed to perform to get to heaven. Now all debts are paid. Because of your honesty and your kindness, you will live happily all the days of your life. Goodbye! I am going to look upon the face of God."

HORSE HOOVES AND CHICKEN FEET

Silvestre Guzmán used to say that when he was a young man, he went to a fiesta one night with his friends. They danced until very late, but on the way home they heard music still coming from somewhere far away.

At first they thought it was coming from the Chávez place; but it wasn't. They kept following the music, which always seemed to be coming from just a little farther off. They walked on, drawn by the lively rhythms of the music, and at last they came to the dance. Each of them chose a partner, and they joined in the fun.

Silvestre was dancing with the prettiest girl there. She had bright flashing eyes and glossy black hair that rippled as she danced. But when Silvestre looked down, he saw that although his partner looked so beautiful, she had chicken feet—scaly claws that should have been scratching around a farmyard, not dancing the night away at a fiesta.

Now he saw that all the women had chicken feet, and all the men had horse hooves. Silvestre signaled frantically to his friends, pointing down at the horse hooves and chicken feet. And one by one they saw what he had seen.

They left the dance in a hurry and walked home in the dawn, thanking their lucky stars for their narrow escape.

For Silvestre and his friends had been dancing with witches. And if Silvestre had not noticed their horse hooves and chicken feet, who knows what would have become of him and his friends?

THE SEVEN OXEN

There were once eight children—seven boys and one girl—who had no father or mother. The two oldest, the girl and a boy, looked after the others, who were only half grown.

Nearby there lived an old witch. When her eyes were open, she was asleep. When her eyes were shut, she was awake.

One day the fire went out in the children's house, and the girl went to the old witch to ask for fire. Her mother had told her before she died, "Never go into the witch's house," but the girl didn't believe that the witch would harm her.

She found the witch standing in the doorway with her eyes closed. She slipped past her, but the witch saw her and chased after her.

The girl ran all the way home and barred the door. The old witch stood at the window and said, "Let me in. Don't be afraid of me." But the girl was afraid, and she would not open the door. Then the witch walked all the way around the house, and where she walked corn and vegetables sprang up behind her.

When the witch was gone, the girl came out and saw everything growing. She said, "Surely the Blessed Virgin sent me all this to feed my brothers." She didn't know that it was the old witch who was responsible.

She harvested all the vegetables and cooked them. When her brothers came home, they were very pleased and sat down to eat. And as they ate, they began to turn into oxen. Her seven brothers turned into seven little blue oxen!

THE SEVEN OXEN

The girl packed herself some provisions and took the oxen out onto the mountain. They would not eat green grass or drink sweet water in the meadows, so she drove them up high where there was dry grass and a spring of mineral water, and there they ate and drank.

Every day the poor sister tended her brothers. And one day a king passed by and said to her, "Girl, will you sell me those little oxen?"

"I will never sell these oxen," she answered. "To take them from me, you would have to kill me."

"But you are too pretty to herd oxen," he said. "You should leave them and come with me."

"No," said the girl, "I will never leave them."

Day after day this went on until one day the king asked, "Why won't you marry me?"

"Because I don't believe anyone else would care for my oxen the way I do," she said.

"I will get my chief cowherd to look after them," the king replied.

And the girl said yes, she would marry him if the oxen were well looked after.

So they were married and the girl went to live in the palace, and her brothers, the oxen, came along, too, so they could be looked after by the king's cowherd.

In time the girl had a baby boy, and the king was crazy about him. But before long the king had to leave his wife and child behind in the palace and go off to war.

One day the queen was gazing down from the balcony of the palace when the old witch came to the well for water. When the witch saw the queen's reflection in the water, she thought it was her own. "I'm too beautiful to be fetching water! I'll break my water jar and go home."

She broke her jar and went home. But when she looked in her mirror, she saw an ugly old lady, same as always.

40

Three times she went for water, and each time it was the same. But the last time she looked up and saw the queen on the balcony. She recognized her at once as the girl who had come to her house to ask for fire.

She climbed up, hand over hand, to the balcony, calling, "I'm coming!" She got closer and closer, and when she reached the balcony, she stuck a pin into the girl's head and turned her into a dove.

The poor queen flew away into the countryside weeping. And the old witch took the queen's baby and tucked herself up in the queen's bed.

When the king came home from the war, he found her in the bed. The room was very dark. "I'm sick," she told him. "I can't bear the light."

The king thought it was his wife. He sent for doctors to cure her, but she never let them see her face. And through all this the girl was flying around in the form of a dove, weeping.

One day the king was walking in his garden very early in the morning, shooing the birds away from the young plants, when his cowherd came to him and said that since dawn a dove had been flying around the oxen and singing this song:

> Listen to my baby cry
> While across the fields I fly.

The king did not know what to make of this. He told the cowherd to catch the dove. The cowherd placed a ball of sticky pine sap in the tree where the bird liked to perch and trapped it that way.

He took the dove to the king, and the king held it in his hand. It was trembling, and the king stroked its feathers to soothe it.

The king carried the bird into the darkened bedroom, to show it to his sick wife.

"Look at this pretty dove," he said.

"Kill it! Kill it! I can't bear it!" shouted the old witch.

But the king went on stroking the bird. He felt a bump on its head, and pulled out the pin.

The dove turned back into his wife before his very eyes.

"What's happening?" he asked.

And the queen told him everything that had happened and how the witch had turned her into a dove and then stolen her baby.

The king dragged the old witch out of bed and rescued the baby, who was almost dead from crying.

And then the queen told the king, "This is the same witch who turned my brothers into oxen."

The king demanded of the witch, "Is it possible to turn the oxen back into boys?"

"Yes," she said.

"Then do so!" he ordered.

The witch was trembling with fear. The little oxen were brought in so that she could remove the spell. She broke a horn from each one, and as she did so, they turned back—not into boys, but into full-grown men.

Then the king ordered wood to be piled up and set on fire, and the old witch was burned up, so she could never harm anyone again.

THE MULE DRIVERS
WHO LOST THEIR FEET

The people from Lagos de Moreno in Jalisco are famous for one thing and one thing alone: Being stupid.

When a prickly pear grew on the roof of the church, they built a ladder so an ox could climb up and eat it. When they first saw a street light, they thought it was the moon on a stick. When a bridge was built over the river, no one used it until a sign was erected, reading, "To get to the other side, put one foot in front of the other."

Anyway, there were once five mule drivers from Lagos de Moreno who were traveling together.

After a while they grew tired, so they sat down in the shade of a tree for a siesta. They stretched out their legs and went to sleep, but when they awoke, their legs were all tangled up.

They couldn't get up, because they had no idea whose legs were whose.

"What shall we do now?" asked one.

"We'll just have to stay here," said another.

So they lay there, wondering what on earth to do. And as they lay there, they grew hungry and thirsty. But still they couldn't get up.

At last a man passed by, and he asked them, "What are you doing there?"

"We can't get up," they answered.

"Why ever not?"

"Because we can't tell whose feet are whose."

The man laughed. "What will you give me if I tell you?"

"Anything you ask!" they said. "If you don't, we will have to stay here and starve to death."

The man took a sharp stick and poked it into a foot.

"Ouch!" said one man.

"That foot is yours," said the stranger. "Pull it out."

He poked the stick into another foot.

"Ouch!" said a second man.

"That foot is yours," said the stranger. "Pull it out."

And he kept on poking until he had found each man's feet for him and they were all untangled.

And the Lagos de Moreno mule drivers were very pleased to have learned that if you want to know whether a foot is yours or not, you should poke it with a stick.

THE TWO MARIAS

There was once a widow who had a daughter named Maria, and a widower who also had a daughter named Maria. Whenever the widower passed the widow's house, she asked him in and gave him bread pudding with honey.

One day the man's daughter asked her father why he did not marry the widow who gave him bread pudding with honey. And her father told her, "Daughter, love starts with bread pudding with honey—but it ends with bread pudding and gall."

But the girl kept on at her father until he agreed to marry the widow.

When they had been married for a while, the father had to leave to tend a flock of sheep. He sent home a lamb for his daughter Maria and a lamb for his stepdaughter Maria, treating them both the same. He did not know that while he was gone, the stepmother and stepsister were being mean and cruel to his daughter. They slaughtered the lamb belonging to his daughter, and sent her to clean it. While she was washing the entrails, a fish snatched them from her hand and swam away with them. Maria began to cry, for she knew she would get the blame. She walked downstream, following the fish, until she came to a house where the Virgin Mary lived. She looked through the door and saw that the Baby Jesus was crying. So she went inside and soothed Him and rocked Him to sleep. And then she began to tidy up the house.

The Virgin Mary came home and saw that Maria had cleaned the house, and she said, "Look up, good girl." Maria looked up, and the Virgin Mary placed a gold star on her forehead.

Then Maria went home. Her stepmother had told the other Maria to watch for her through the window. When she saw the star on Maria's forehead, the stepsister shouted, "She's coming! She's coming! And she's shining like a star!"

Her mother looked out the window and said, "Where would a good-for-nothing like that get a star? She must have stuck a piece of tin on her forehead."

When the girl got home, her stepmother asked, "What took you so long?"

Maria told her how the fish had stolen the entrails and how the Virgin Mary had placed a star on her forehead.

"A likely story!" said the stepmother, and she tried to cut the star off Maria's brow. But she could not, which made her even angrier than before.

So the woman slaughtered her own daughter's lamb and sent her to the river to clean it. The same fish came and stole away the entrails, and the daughter screamed and cursed at it.

"I suppose I had better follow it," she grumbled, and she set off downstream, dragging her feet, until she reached the Virgin Mary's house.

Inside the house she could hear the Baby Jesus crying. "What an awful noise," she said. And she went indoors, spanked the Baby Jesus to shut Him up, and threw things all over the place. As she left, she met the Virgin Mary coming home. "What do you think you're doing, going off walking and leaving your child alone?" she asked.

And the Virgin Mary said, "Look up." Maria looked up, and two horns sprouted from the sides of her head.

The girl went home in a rage. When she got there, she told her mother everything that had happened, and the mother was so angry that she took a knife and cut the horns off. But they just grew back, even bigger than before.

THE TWO MARIAS

The stepmother was furious. She said to her stepdaughter, "What are you looking at? Go and make yourself useful—fetch some wood for the fire."

While Maria was gathering firewood, the king's son rode by, saw the gold star gleaming on her forehead, and fell madly in love with her.

"Would you like to marry me?" he asked.

"Yes," she replied.

Maria took the wood back to the house and asked her stepmother if she could marry the king's son.

"Yes," said the stepmother, "but not until you have prepared a table for the wedding feast, filled with every kind of food." And then she said, "I expect you to have it ready by the time I get back from my walk. Otherwise, you cannot marry the prince."

Maria just sat in the doorway and cried. How could she ever prepare a table with every kind of food in such a short time?

A woman came by and asked her, "Why are you crying?"

Maria told her, and the woman said, "Don't worry." Maria wiped the tears from her eyes, and when she looked up, the table was ready.

Maria wasn't sure, but she thought maybe the woman was the same one who had placed the gold star on her forehead.

When the stepmother came home and found the table all ready, she asked, "What's been going on here?"

Maria told her everything, and that just made the stepmother angrier than ever. "I will not let you marry the prince unless you fill twelve mattresses with little birds' feathers."

Maria went off to the hillside crying. As she sat weeping beneath a pine tree, a bird with a whistle in its beak came and said, "Don't worry. Blow this whistle, and all the little birds in the world will come and give their feathers to help you."

The bird flew off, and Maria blew the whistle. Sure enough, all the little birds of the world came flying to her, and each one gave her a feather until she had enough to fill the twelve mattresses.

Maria carried the twelve mattresses home and gave them to her stepmother. That made her so mad! "I will not let you marry the prince until you bring me ten bottles full of little birds' tears!" she said.

Maria walked sadly back to the hillside. She did not know what to do. But the same bird came back and said, "Blow the whistle again, and the birds will return and shed their tears to help you."

She blew the whistle, and once more all the little birds of the world came flying to her. They started to cry, and their tears dropped into the ten bottles. When the bottles were full, the birds flew away.

Maria carried the ten bottles of birds' tears to her stepmother. The wicked woman was even angrier than before, and this time she told Maria outright, "I will never let you marry the prince. If anyone is going to marry the prince, it shall be my own daughter, with her fine horns."

And the stepmother locked Maria in a dark cellar and told her, "You can stay there until you have learned your place."

Soon the king's son came calling at the house, asking for Maria with the gold star, so that he could marry her.

"She has run away, the ungrateful wretch," said the stepmother. "She has gone to join her father. But her beautiful stepsister is here." And she called out to her daughter, "Maria, come and meet the prince!"

Now, there was a cat in the house who had always been treated lovingly by Maria with the gold star and cruelly by Maria with the horns. And the cat sang out, "Gold Star is locked in the cellar! Gold Star is locked in the cellar."

The prince heard the cat and ordered the stepmother to set Maria free. And when they opened the cellar door, it was not dark in there at all, for golden light was spilling from the star on Maria's forehead, and it was as bright as day.

The prince took Maria to the palace and married her, and they lived happily together for many years.

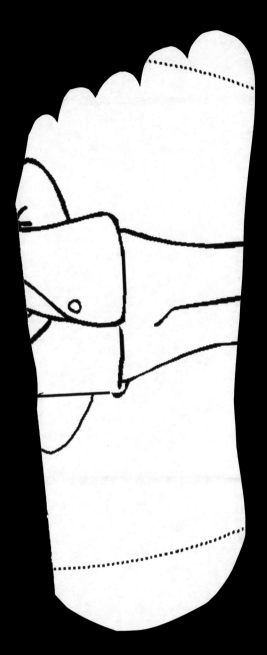

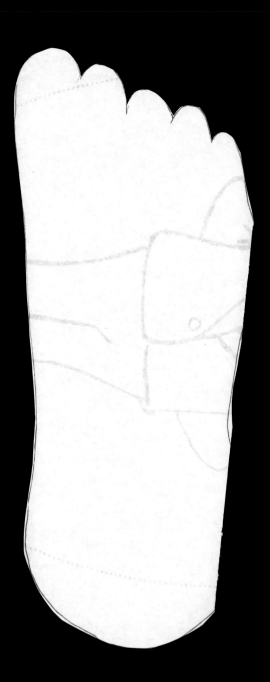

THE PRIEST WHO HAD
A GLIMPSE OF GLORY

Once there was a priest who longed to see the glory of God.

One day as he was putting on his vestments before going to say Mass, he sighed, "Oh, Lord! If only I could have one small glimpse!"

He stepped outside, and in the air he heard the song of a little bird. It was so liquid and so lovely that the priest stared up at the sky, hoping to see the bird. He stood there, transfixed by the beauty of its song.

Then he shook himself and hurried to the church. But when he got there, all he found was a ruin. There was no church and no altar. Just a pile of stones.

He stopped some passersby. "What's happened to the church?" he asked.

"The church?" they answered. "The story goes that long ago there was a priest there. But he vanished between the sacristy and the church and was never seen again. So the church was left to fall down."

And then the priest understood. While he was enjoying just one small glimpse of glory, many years passed. Only eternity is long enough to see God's glory in all its splendor.

THE BRAVE WIDOW

There was a young wife who had a son. When her husband died, she left her son with his grandmother, dressed herself in men's clothes, and went off to see the world.

She came to a mountain where two hunters were making their camp. They invited her to join them; they had no idea she was a woman.

The widow stayed behind at the camp to prepare the meal while the others went out hunting. They warned her, "There's someone who sneaks into the camp and steals our food, but we don't know who it is." The young widow said she would stay and keep watch.

Soon after the men had gone, an old woman came to the camp and started to steal the food. The young widow picked up a club and chased her off; the old woman scuttled down a hole that was near the camp.

When the two hunters returned, the young widow said, "It was an old woman! I chased her with my club, but she escaped down that hole."

"How will we wangle her out?" said one.

"Let's make a rope out of hide and climb down after her," said the other.

So they made a rope, and the first man started to climb down into the hole. Soon the others lost sight of him in the darkness. Then they heard a scream, and the rope started shaking and swaying as the man shinned back up it as fast as he could.

"What's wrong?" they asked him.

"I just got scared," he said.

So the second man climbed down, hand over hand. But the same thing happened with him—as soon as he got near the bottom of the hole, he lost his nerve and hauled himself back up to the top, trembling with fear.

"Did you see anything down there?" asked the widow.

"I saw a light," he said.

So the widow took her cudgel and climbed down the rope. When she reached the bottom, she too saw the light. When nothing happened, she made her way toward it. There she found three beautiful girls, who shrank from her in fear.

"What are you doing here?" one of them asked. "Can't you see we are under a spell? We are captives of Judas and his old wife, who feeds us."

"Don't be afraid," said the young widow. "I will free you, even if it costs me my life."

"How, sir?" asked the captive girl. "Judas stole us away from our father the king, and no one has been able to rescue us."

But the young widow just told them not to worry, she would free them.

She led the princesses to the bottom of the hole and showed them how to climb up the rope of hide. One by one, the three princesses climbed up to the top.

When they saw three lovely princesses emerging from the hole, the hunters were amazed at their luck. Quickly they pulled up the rope, leaving the young widow stranded at the bottom. They didn't give her a thought; they were too busy arguing about which of the princesses they would marry.

The widow felt very sad when she saw how she had been abandoned. She turned around and saw the old woman coming after her, shouting, "What have you done here, thief? You've stolen our three princesses! Judas will catch you and eat you!"

The widow raised her club and struck the old woman down.

Along came Judas, bellowing, "I smell human meat! Give me human meat to eat!"

Then Judas saw the young widow. "You have stolen my three princesses," he roared. "I will eat you up!"

The widow raised her club and struck the first blow. Judas dodged it, and the club glanced off his head, knocking off an ear.

Judas came at her, and the widow flung her rosary around his neck. He fell to the floor, helpless.

"Set me free!" he begged.

"It is not I who is holding you down," she said. "But I can free you if you promise to help me escape."

"I promise," said Judas.

"Truly?"

"Word of a king," said Judas, for he *was* the king of the underworld.

The widow took back her rosary, and Judas showed her a way out to the world above.

"I have kept my promise," he said. "Can I have my ear back?"

"Not yet," said the widow. "I may need it."

She left Judas and headed for the city. Her son was there, but he did not know that his mother had returned. The two hunters were also there, married to the two older princesses. And the youngest princess was there, looking longingly from a window and wishing the handsome young man who had rescued her would come and claim her as his bride.

When the widow came to the king's palace, the guards would not let her in. But the youngest princess saw her rescuer and told the king to let him in, for he was to be her husband.

The king told the guards to let the stranger in. The widow told him how she had rescued the princesses from Judas's spell and showed him the ear as proof. The two hunters, who had told the king that *they* had rescued the princesses, turned pale when they saw the ear. They knew that the widow was telling the truth.

"Welcome! Welcome!" said the king. "You rescued my daughters, and you shall marry the youngest one."

"No," said the widow.

"What's this?" said the king. "A brave man like you, refusing to marry my daughter? Why? You have won her; she is yours."

The widow replied, "I have a son who is dearer to me than my own heart, and I would like him to marry the princess."

"But why?" asked the king.

"Because I cannot marry a woman," she said.

"Why not?"

"Because I am a woman," she replied.

"I don't believe that the person who freed my daughters from Judas, king of the underworld, is a woman," said the king.

"But nevertheless I am," she said.

"Do you swear it, on pain of death?" he asked.

"Yes," she said.

"Then fetch your son, and he shall marry my daughter and be my heir."

The widow's son was brought to the palace, and the youngest princess took to him straight away. So they were married at once.

Then the king asked the widow, "What shall we do with those traitors who left you in the cave? Say the word, and I shall put them to death."

"No," said the widow. "It is true that they betrayed me, but to execute them would also punish their new wives, who have done no wrong. Let them make your two older daughters happy; that is the best course."

The king agreed to live and let live, so long as the two hunters kept their wives happy.

Then he said to the widow, "When next I go to war, I shall make you captain of all my armies, for you are braver and wiser than any man in my kingdom."

THE ENDLESS TALE

Once there was a very rich man who had a daughter who was a wonderful storyteller. He enjoyed her stories so much that he told her he would never let her marry, for he wanted her to tell him a story every day. He loved to listen to her weave her tales, and he had only one complaint. "Your stories are too short," he said. "I wish you could tell me a story that lasted for a month."

"A story that went on for a whole month would be boring," she answered.

"Not to me," he said. "I would love it. I wouldn't be bored. Why, if anyone could tell a story long enough to bore me, I would gladly let him marry you, even though it would mean him taking you away from me."

When the young men heard that, they all tried to invent really long stories, for the rich man's daughter was not just a good storyteller, she was also a great beauty. But although some of them started well, none of them could keep their stories going.

Now, the rich man's daughter had her eye on a poor boy, and she took him aside and said, "When you tell your story to my father, this is what you should say . . ."

So the poor boy came their house, and he said, "There was once a man who was very rich and very wise who lived near a mountain. Thinking that a famine might come, he harvested all his corn and hid it in a vast cave in the mountain, behind a door that he locked securely so that no one could come and steal the corn. But

he did not notice a tiny crack in the door, just big enough for an ant to slip through. When he had gone, an ant came, and stole a single grain of corn."

The poor boy took a breath and continued, "And then the ant came back and stole another grain of corn, and then another grain of corn, and then another, and then another, and then another. . . ."

After the poor boy had been telling his story for two days, the rich man could not bear it any more. "Your story will bore me to death," he said. "Stop!"

"But there is much more," said the poor boy. "This story is quite long enough to last for a whole month, or even longer."

The rich man laughed. "You win," he said. "You may marry my daughter."

So the poor boy and the rich man's daughter were married, and neither of them ever told a boring story again.

CINDER JUAN

There were once three brothers who lived happily with their mother and father. But first the mother died and then the father, and that was when the trouble began.

Their father left the house to the three brothers, divided like this: three roof beams to the oldest son, two roof beams to the middle son, and one roof beam to the youngest son, whose name was Juan.

Now, Juan was perfectly happy about this. "One roof beam is enough for me," he said. But his brothers and their wives were jealous that he should have even a single beam over his head.

"That roof beam should be yours by rights. You are the eldest son," said one wife.

"Why should your older brother have three beams, while you have only two? It's not fair," said the other wife.

The only thing that the two wives agreed on was that Juan had no right at all to his part of the house. "His father may have left him a roof beam," they said, "but he never mentioned the roof."

Juan had taken a job as a servant to a rich man who lived nearby, and while he was out, his sisters-in-law removed all the crosswise wooden slats that formed the roof at Juan's end of the house and burned them.

When Juan returned to eat his tortilla, which was all he had for supper that night and breakfast the next day, his roof was gone. When he lay down to sleep, he was looking straight up at the stars.

CINDER JUAN

The next night, while Juan was preparing his tortilla, he heard a meow. A stray tomcat had slipped over the wall of his room to join him. "Hello, kitty," said Juan. "Are you hungry?" And he shared his tortilla with the cat.

That night it was very cold, and Juan spread the warm ashes from his fire over the floor, to make a warm bed for himself and his new friend the cat.

In the morning, the two sisters-in-law told their husbands, "We can't bear to share a house with that dirty brother of yours." And they started calling him Cinder Juan.

One night the cat began scratching and digging in the cinders. "Stop that!" said Juan, but the cat just yowled at him and carried on digging.

The noise woke Juan's sisters-in-law. "Have you ever heard such a racket?" they tut-tutted.

"Perhaps Cinder Juan is being murdered in his bed," said one.

"That's too much to hope for," said the other.

And the sisters-in-law went back to sleep.

The cat kept on scratching at the earth floor until at last he dug up a little wooden box with a silver key. Juan opened it, and inside he found a piece of paper. "I wonder what it says on this paper?" said Juan. But he could not read a word.

As soon as the sun rose the next day, Juan took the paper to the lawyer who had dealt with his father's will and asked him what it said. "It says there is a chest full of gold buried beneath the floor of your room, which is your father's legacy to you," the lawyer said. "Your father knew that your brothers would try to cheat you. My advice to you is to dig up the money and go to live somewhere else. Otherwise, your brothers will try to take it from you."

So Juan and his cat dug up the chest full of gold in the night and went to live in the city, without telling Juan's brothers anything about it.

CINDER JUAN

Juan's brothers had no idea where he had gone. But they had suspicious minds, and one said to the other, "I bet he's up to no good." So they decided to look for him.

They asked everyone they met whether they had met a poor man named Cinder Juan, but no one had heard of him.

"The only Juan we know is the rich man who has moved to the city," they said, "the one who is so friendly with the priest and always so generous to the poor."

The brothers decided they had to go to the city to investigate. When they arrived in the market square, they heard a girl shouting, "Who'll buy my talking parrot? Who'll buy?"

"Can this parrot really talk?" the brothers asked.

"Talk? This bird can talk the hind legs off a donkey," the girl replied.

So the brothers bought the parrot. They found out Juan was living next door to the church and left the parrot on the windowsill of Juan's house, instructing it to find out everything it could about Juan and fly back and tell them.

When Juan noticed the parrot, he said, "Hello, bird, what are you doing here?"

"I have flown away from my brothers, who were jealous of me," said the bird.

"Me, too," said Juan.

The two fell into conversation, and Juan told the parrot all about the chest of gold.

When night fell, the parrot flew back to the market square and told the brothers what he had heard.

Now, there was an old woman who lived in a wretched little hut near the market, and she heard everything the parrot and the brothers said. Juan had often given her a coin or two. So she went to him and warned him that his brothers meant to do him harm. But because he had such a good heart, he would not believe her. However, the cat listened to every word she said.

In the middle of the night the cat tried to wake Juan, shouting, "Fire! Fire! Run for your life! Your jealous brothers have set the house on fire!"

But Juan would not wake up.

The cat ran next door to the church and rang the church bell, clinging to the bell rope with his claws and swaying wildly as the bell rang out its warning: *Fire! Fire!*

That woke Juan, and he fled from the house.

Juan and the cat took refuge in the priest's house.

"How can I ever thank you?" Juan asked the cat.

"Pay the priest to say a mass for the soul of your father and a mass for the soul of your mother," said the cat. "That will be thanks enough."

Then the cat told Juan, "You will be safe here. But never open the door, especially if the priest is not here, and ask the priest not to tell anyone you are here. Otherwise, your brothers may find you and try to kill you."

"But what shall I do about my brothers?"

"You can leave them to me," said the cat. "Your brothers are two trees that have grown crooked—but I shall straighten them out."

So Juan stayed in the priest's house and refused to answer the door to anyone in case his treacherous brothers had come back to murder him. As the cat had instructed him, he paid the priest to say a mass for the soul of his father and a mass for the soul of his mother.

When the masses had been said, the cat returned, wrapped in a cloth as white as snow, and told Juan that now he had spent his inheritance in the way that had been intended, he need fear his brothers no more. "Thank you for doing what I asked. Now I can enter heaven," said the cat.

Juan was confused. He looked at the priest, and the priest said, "This cat is the soul of your father."

CINDER JUAN

The cat looked deep into Juan's eyes, and Juan knew that it was true. And then the cat raised a paw in farewell, saying, "I cannot stay with you. I must return to God."

Juan was never troubled by his wicked brothers again. The old woman from the market saw them running out of town as fast as their legs could carry them, but even Juan's jealous sisters-in-law never found out the full story. One of the brothers babbled on about a talking parrot, the other about a talking cat. And the sisters-in-law agreed, "Our husbands have even less sense than Cinder Juan."

THE STORYTELLER'S PARTING WORDS

Once there was a cat
with paws made of rag
and eyes in the back
of its head . . . so it's said.
Do you want me to tell it again?

NOTES ON THE STORIES

The AT numbers in the following notes refer to a widely used classification of international folktale types, which can be found in *The Types of the Folktale* by Antti Aarne and Stith Thompson (AT stands for Aarne-Thompson). Readers who wish to pursue these types across cultures may do so most easily by consulting D. L. Ashliman, *A Guide to Folktales in the English Language.* Also organized on the same principle are: *Type and Motif Index of the Folktales of England and North America* by Ernest W. Baughman; *Index of Spanish Folktales* by Ralph Steele Boggs; *The Types of the Folktale in Cuba, Puerto Rico, the Dominican Republic, and Spanish South America* by Terrence Leslie Hansen; and *Index of Mexican Folktales* by Stanley L. Robe. Most of the individual collections discussed here include indexes of tale types keyed to the Aarne-Thompson numbers. As in the Bibliography, the spelling of the words "folktale" and "folklore" has been standardized throughout in the titles of books and articles.

THE FLEA

This story was collected from Enrique Valdés in Antonito, Colorado, by Juan B. Rael; it is tale 258 in his *Cuentos Españoles de Colorado y de Nuevo Méjico.* Like all the other stories in this book, it is both typically Mexican and recognizably a variant on an international theme. In this case, it is a version of AT 329, "Hiding from the Devil." In another story collected by Rael (tale 261, "Don Jacinto"), it is indeed the Devil, not a magician, from whom the hero hides. On the first night he climbs to the moon with the aid of an eagle he has previously helped, but is discovered; on the second night he sleeps inside a fish, but is discovered; on the third night he sleeps in the form of an ant, underneath the

sheepskin where a captive princess is sleeping. This time he is not discovered, and is able to join forces with the princess to slay the Devil. There is another version of "The Flea" in Teresa Pijoan de Van Etten, *Spanish-American Folktales*. She heard it in oral tradition from a Señor Jaramillo while stringing chilis—a perfect example of the way storytelling dances in and out of everyday life in the Hispanic Southwest.

THE STORY OF THE SUN
AND THE MOON

This story was collected in the pueblo of Azqueltán in the state of Jalisco, Mexico, a village of the Tepehuane (or Tepecano) people, by J. Alden Mason in 1912, and published in his essay "Four Mexican-Spanish Fairytales from Azqueltán, Jalisco" in the *Journal of American Folklore*. It is the only example in this book of a story from Spanish tradition incorporated into Native American storytelling, but it could be matched by many more, especially from the Pueblos of the Southwest. Interestingly, while the Native Mexican storytelling tradition—represented at its purest in Robert M. Laughlin's marvellous collection of Tzotzil texts from Zinacantán, *Of Cabbages and Kings*—has absorbed elements of Hispanic storytelling, there has been little traffic in the other direction. Hispanic narrators rarely show any Indian influence.

"The Story of the Sun and of the Moon" is a version of AT 400, "The Man on a Quest for His Lost Wife," with elements of AT 313, "The Girl as Helper in the Hero's Flight." AT 400 and its counterpart AT 425, "The Search for the Lost Husband," are extremely popular in Mexican tradition.

Versions in which a girl searches for her lost husband can be very similar to those in which a man searches for his lost love. For instance, the story "The Mountains of Mogollón" (tale 156 in Rael, *Cuentos Españoles de Colorado y de Nuevo Méjico*), is very like "The Story of the Sun and the Moon." The principal difference is that the heroine is searching for her husband, who had been turned into a frog until her mother treacherously burned his frog skin while he slept in human form. She has the same encounter with the three brothers, and acquires their magic objects in the same way, and visits the moon, the morning star, the sun, and finally the wind in her search. Like the hero of our story, she uses the magic objects to succeed in her quest. This story does not, however, have the incident (typical of AT 313) of the "obstacle flight," in which the hero and heroine make their escape by dropping objects behind them that become barriers to their pursuer.

THE TAILOR WHO SOLD HIS SOUL TO THE DEVIL

Folktales in which a crafty human outwits the Devil (or an ogre) are always popular. In some stories the Devil is set an impossible task, such as turning a curly hair into a straight one; in others the Devil proves incompetent at some human skill, such as sewing, that proves to be more difficult than it looks.

This particular story, AT 1096, "The Tailor and the Ogre in a Sewing Contest," has two variants in Mexican tradition. The version I have used is story 46 in Paredes, *Folktales of Mexico.* It was collected in 1948 by Vicente T. Mendoza and Virginia Rodríguez Rivera de Mendoza from Petra Guzmán Barrón, and was first published in Mendoza, *Folklore de San Pedro Piedra Gorda, Zacatecas.*

Story 180 in Wheeler, *Tales from Jalisco, Mexico*, is a longer and more complex treatment of the same theme. In it the devil disguises himself as a farmer and commissions the tailor to make him a suit. When the tailor steals the leftover fabric, the Devil claims him. He is about to carry the tailor to hell when the tailor's wife challenges him to a sewing contest, with the same result. The Devil departs, muttering, "What a woman! More devilish than the Devil is!"

This story has been found more frequently in northern than southern Europe: there are 150 Swedish versions, but none, so far as I know, from mainland Spain, though there are many Spanish folktales about tailors (see Boggs, *Index of Spanish Folktales*, types 1710–19). Even so, it is likely that the Mexican versions originated in Spanish tradition.

In my retelling I have added the "seven years" motif (in an English version, the Devil gives the tailor a bag of gold that can never be emptied) and also the sly touch that it is the tailor who threads the Devil's needle with the unworkably long thread.

THE HOG

This story is 54 in Rael, *Cuentos Españoles de Colorado y de Nuevo Méjico.* It was collected from Presciliano López in Del Norte, Colorado,

in 1930. This little anecdote is an internationally known tale type, AT 1792, "The Stingy Parson and the Slaughtered Pig." It is told all over Europe, including Spain; there is a Catalan version in J. Amades, *Folklore de Catalunya*. (1950). A literary version was included in the *Decameron* of Boccaccio (1349–51). In an amusing Ozark variant in Vance Randolph's *The Devil's Pretty Daughter*, the "hog" is not a pig but a barrel of whiskey; other North American texts are closer to the standard form.

PEDRO THE TRICKSTER

This story is based on tale 274 in Juan B. Rael, *Cuentos Españoles de Colorado y de Nuevo Méjico,* which was collected from Josefa Chalifú in Costilla, New Mexico. However, I have added some touches from other versions of this most popular of Mexican tales. Rael's collection alone contains sixteen narratives about Pedro de Ordimalas (or Urdemalas) and ten further related tales, and there are others in almost every collection of Mexican tales; Aurelio M. Espinosa includes a section of continental Spanish tales of "Pedro el de Malas" or "Pedro Malasartes" in his *Cuentos Populares Españoles,* with useful comparative notes. The variants most closely related to the version here are listed in Robe's *Index of Mexican Folktales* under type 330, "The Smith Outwits the Devil." This is a very popular international tale type; there are, for instance, 359 Irish versions. It has been collected elsewhere in the United States, notably as one of the "Jack" tales in the Appalachians; in the version in Richard Chase, *Grandfather Tales*, the hero, Wicked John, banned from both heaven and hell, becomes the "Jacky-my-lantern," the will-o'-the-wisp, and the same fate befalls him in the African American version, "Jacky-My-Lantern," in the Uncle Remus tales. In some Mexican versions—for instance that in J. Alden Mason, "Folktales of the Tepecanos"—it is made clear that Pedro has been turned into a font for holy water, as in the doorway of a church. The Mexican characterization of Death (La Muerte) as female can be seen in stories such as "La Muerte" in Robe, *Hispanic Folktales from New Mexico,* or "Godmother Death" in Glazer, *Flour from Another Sack*.

THE SHADOW

This story was told by Benigna Vigil of Santa Cruz, New Mexico, to José Manuel Espinosa, and is printed as story 42 in his *Spanish Folktales*

from New Mexico. She was a fine storyteller and also narrated "The Two Marias" and "The Seven Oxen." Espinosa gives the story the title "El Muerto Agradecido": "The Grateful Dead Man." It is an example of AT 506, "The Rescued Princess," one of a group of related "Grateful Dead" tale types. The most well-known "Grateful Dead" story is that of Tobias and the angel in the Book of Tobit.

There is a very similar story, "Don Juanito," in Rael, *Cuentos Españoles de Colorado y de Nuevo Méjico,* as well as an interesting variant in which the hero, Bernardo, rescues a girl held captive by Indians and is helped by the soul of the dead man in the form of a coyote. This latter version roots this story, of Spanish origin, firmly in the American Southwest. Mexican parallels can be found in tales 116 and 117 in Wheeler, *Tales from Jalisco, Mexico.* In the first of these the girl has been stolen by the police, and the helper is a "white shadow"; in the second the girls are enslaved by a Moor, and the helper is a crow.

Similar stories have also been collected in Puerto Rico, Chile, and the Dominican Republic.

HORSE HOOVES AND CHICKEN FEET

This tale is story 7 in Paredes, *Folktales of Mexico.* It was collected by Vicente T. Mendoza and Virginia Rodríguez Rivera de Mendoza from Aureliano Guzmán, who learned the tale from his father, Silvestre. It was first published in Mendoza, *Folklore de San Pedro Piedra Gorda, Zacatecas.*

This is a very common tale in Spanish America. Sometimes the witches have goose feet, not chicken feet; where the story is told about a girl, she usually sees her partner's hoofs and realizes she is dancing with the Devil. The story is almost always told as true. Mark Glazer includes an excellent version, "Devil at the Dance," in *Flour from Another Sack,* in which the young man has "a horse's hoof and a chicken's foot." In this version the girl faints away, is taken to the hospital by ambulance, and dies from the shock. It was collected from a 12-year-old Mexican American girl who had heard it from a classmate; Glazer notes, "This story became very popular in April, 1979 in Rio Grande Valley schools. Most of her classmates believed this story." See also story 32 in Robe, *Mexican Tales and Legends from Veracruz,* and for a twist on the theme, story 500 in Rael, *Cuentos Españoles de Colorado y de Nuevo Méjico.*

THE SEVEN OXEN

This story was collected by José Manuel Espinosa from 52-year-old Benigna Vigil in Santa Cruz, New Mexico, in 1931, and is printed as story 10 in his *Spanish Folktales from New Mexico.* Espinosa recorded several similar tales, including one which is much like this except there are only three brothers and they never regain their human form. In his *Index of Spanish Folktales,* Ralph S. Boggs lists the tale of the seven oxen as type 327*D, considering it a variant of the story of "The Children and the Ogre," but it is probably best considered as a separate, typically Spanish, variant of AT 451, "The Maiden Who Seeks Her Brothers," which mixes motifs from various tale types. In a version called "The Little Oxen," in Aurora Lucero-White Lea's *Literary Folklore of the Hispanic Southwest,* for instance, there are resemblances to the story of Snow White. The story "The Golden Star" in Rael's *Cuentos Españoles de Colorado y de Nuevo Méjico* is a mixture of "Cinderella," "The Prince as a Bird," and "The Three Oranges." There are a further four fine versions in Rael (nos. 179–182), strikingly similar to the Espinosa texts; Rael classifies them as variants of AT 408, "The Three Oranges." In Puerto Rico, where the story tells of sisters rather than brothers who are turned into oxen, Hansen classifies the tale as 452*B, "The Sisters as Oxen"; apart from the change of gender of the enchanted siblings, the tale is almost identical to "The Seven Oxen." In his *Index of Mexican Folktales,* Stanley L. Robe adopts Hansen's suggested type for all such stories and gives a detailed analysis of its variations.

THE MULE DRIVERS
WHO LOST THEIR FEET

This story was collected in 1947 by Stanley L. Robe in Tepatitlán, Jalisco, from María de Jesús Navarro de Aceves and printed as story 118 in Robe's *Mexican Tales and Legends from Los Altos.* The book contains a number of other stories about the legendary stupidity of the inhabitants of Lagos de Moreno. The story is also in Parades, *Folktales of Mexico,* where it is mistakenly attributed to another narrator. It is a version of an internationally told tale, AT 1288, "Numskulls Cannot Find Their Own Legs."

Most countries have villages or towns where the inhabitants are supposed to be simpletons; England has around fifty, including Idbury, where I live. It is said that the inhabitants of Idbury, having noticed that it was always good weather when the cuckoo was here, tried to pen the cuckoo in so that they could enjoy summer all the year round; one of the local fields is still called Cuckoo Pen.

THE TWO MARIAS

This story is no. 5 in José Manuel Espinosa, *Spanish Folktales from New Mexico;* it was collected from Benigna Vigil in 1931. Espinosa also publishes a similar tale, "Gold Star," in which instead of the three tests in our story, the Virgin Mary gives Gold Star beautiful clothes. She wears these to church, where the prince falls in love with her. In classic Cinderella style, he picks up her slipper as she leaves. Our tale is a mixture of AT 511, "One-Eye, Two-Eyes, Three-Eyes" (part of the Cinderella cycle), and AT 480, "The Kind and Unkind Girls," two tale types that often intertwine. In other Mexican versions, the unkind sister is punished with even more humiliating signs of her unworthiness than horns, such as burro dung on her forehead (as, for instance, in "Cinder-Mary" in Mason, "Four Mexican-Spanish Fairytales from Azqueltán, Jalisco," or stories 68 and 69 in Robe, *Mexican Tales and Legends from Los Altos*). The Virgin Mary appears in the "fairy godmother" role in a number of Mexican versions, including stories 106–8 in Rael, *Cuentos Españoles de Colorado y de Nueva Méjico.* In a version in Wheeler, *Tales from Jalisco, Mexico,* the helper is Saint Peter. The father's rather gloomy proverb before marriage rhymes in the original: "Primero son sopitas de miel y luego serán sopitas de hiel."

THE PRIEST WHO HAD
A GLIMPSE OF GLORY

I have based this tale on story 38 in Paredes, *Folktales of Mexico;* it was collected by Virginia Rodríguez Rivera de Mendoza in 1948 from Petra Guzmán Barrón (who also told the story of "The Tailor Who Sold His Soul to the Devil"). A similar text is included in Mendoza, *Folklore de San Pedro Pieda Gorda, Zacatecas.* The tale type here, AT 471A, "The Monk and the Bird," is widespread, especially in Catholic countries. A famous version was contributed to *The Amulet, or Christian and Literary Remembrancer* in 1827 by the Irish collector T. Crofton Croker, and can easily be found in W. B. Yeats, *Fairy Tales of Ireland*. In a Spanish tale in A. de Llano Roza de Ampudia, *Cuentos Asturianos* (1925), a shepherd strolls into heaven and stays there for 300 years, though he thinks he has only been there a short time. An Islamic equivalent, "The King Who Wanted to See Paradise," collected from a Pathan tribesman in what is now Pakistan, was included in Andrew Lang's *The Orange Fairy Book*.

THE BRAVE WIDOW

This unusual tale was collected from Sixto Chávez from Vaughn, New Mexico, in 1931. It is tale 21 in José Manuel Espinosa, *Spanish Folktales from New Mexico*. That the leading character is female only slightly disguises the fact that this story is a version of what is perhaps the single most popular fairy tale in Hispanic tradition, "Juan Oso" ("John the Bear"). This is a specifically Spanish twist on the international type AT 301, "The Three Stolen Princesses." José Manuel Espinosa's book contains five versions, of which this is the only one with a heroine. The "shift of sex" motif is fundamental to several tale types (notably AT 514, "The Shift of Sex"; AT 881A, "The Abandoned Bride Disguised As a Man"; AT 882, "The Wager on the Wife's Chastitity"; and AT 884, "The Forsaken Fiancée"). A continental Spanish tale on this theme is "El Oricuerno," tale 155 in Aurelio M. Espinosa, *Cuentos Populares Españoles*.

The motif of a girl or woman disguised as a man is found in a number of Mexican stories, including tales 1, 70, 71, and 72 in José Manuel Espinosa, *Spanish Folktales from New Mexico;* tale 107 in Paul Radin and Aurelio M. Espinosa, *El Folklore de Oaxaca;* tales 50, 71, and 72 in Wheeler, *Tales from Jalisco, Mexico;* tale 41 in George M. Foster, "Sierra Popoluca Folklore and Beliefs"; and tales 10, 11, and 126–35 in Rael, *Cuentos Españoles de Colorado y de Nuevo Méjico.* In many of these tales the disguised woman distinguishes herself by her bravery; for instance, in tale 130 in Rael, a wife who is unjustly cast out by her husband dresses as a man, joins the king's army, and fights with such bravery that she is rewarded by the king, who allows her to return to her home village dressed as a king, where she sets all to rights.

For a typical version of "John the Bear" and a discussion of this type, see John O. West, *Mexican-American Folklore*, pp. 101–4. For a most unusual one adapted to Native American tradition, see "The Four Brothers," story 81 in Elsie Clews Parsons, *Taos Tales*; story 78 in that volume, "The Faithful Wife and the Woman Warrior," probably also derives from Spanish origins.

THE ENDLESS TALE

This tale is based on a story 73 in Rael, *Cuentos Españoles de Colorado y de Nuevo Méjico,* which was collected from Valentín Suazo in Abiquiu, New Mexico. It is a version of AT 2301A, "Making the King Lose Patience." I have taken the liberty of giving the rich man's daughter a more active role. A similar tale, in which the young man's story involves an ant carrying grains of sand across a river, can be found in Richard Garnica Ornelas's M.A. thesis, "Folk Tales of the Spanish Southwest" (1962). Versions of this story have been collected across the United States—in Missouri, Mississippi, Pennsylvania, Idaho, Indiana, and Kentucky—and it appears to have been carried into American tradition, one telling at a time, by storytellers from Germany, France, Ireland, and England, as well as from Spain. Another endless tale from Mexican American tradition (story 22 in Zunser, "A New Mexican Village") tells of a man who builds a bridge so that his flock of sheep can cross the river one at a time to reach the corral. The storyteller pauses, and when the listener asks, "Well, what happened?" he replies, "Wait for the sheep to cross the river."

CINDER JUAN

This mysterious tale is story 242 in Juan B. Rael, *Cuentos Españoles de Colorado y de Nuevo Méjico;* it was recorded from Eva Martínez in Conejos, Colorado. A lively retelling by Joe Hayes is the title tale of his collection *Everyone Knows Gato Pinto,* and I have borrowed from Mr. Hayes the charming image of the cat swinging from the church bell rope to alert Juan to the fire. The story is a variant of AT 545, "The Cat as Helper," with a specifically Mexican American flavor both in the setting and in the religious overtones; the traditional division of inherited property by vigas, or roof beams, is a particularly authentic touch. Stanley Robe in his *Index of Mexican Folktales* classifies it as 545*F, of which this version is the only example. Robe lists seven more typical versions of "Puss in Boots," including two in Rael's collection (tales 240 and 241). Helpful animals in folktales are often either explicitly or implicitly understood to be the returning soul either of a grateful stranger or, as here, of the hero or heroine's father or mother.

THE STORYTELLER'S PARTING WORDS

This nonsense verse (from Aurelio M. Espinosa, "New-Mexican Spanish Folklore VII: More Folktales") is in the tradition of "put-off" rhymes by means of which storytellers evade requests for further stories. Because it ends with the question, "Do you want me to tell it again?" the rhyme can be endless repeated in a round, and classified as AT 2320, "Round."

Other versions of this formula tale can be found in Paredes, *Folktales of Mexico*, and Parsons, "Folklore from Santa Ana Xalmimilulco Pueblo, Mexico"; it was first recorded in Albert S. Gatschet, "Popular Rimes from Mexico" in 1889.

The most famous of all such put-offs is the English rhyme quoted in Charles Dickens, *Our Mutual Friend* (1864–5):

> I'll tell you a story
> Of Jack a Manory,
> And now my story's begun;
> I'll tell you another
> Of Jack and his brother,
> And now my story is done.

BIBLIOGRAPHY

The old-fashioned spellings "folk-lore" and "folk-tale" have been standardized to "folklore" and "folktale."

Aarne, Antti, and Stith Thompson. *The Types of the Folktale.* Helsinki: Suomalainen Tiedeakatemia, 2nd rev., 1961. Folklore Fellows Communications, no. 184.

Aiken, Riley. "A Pack Load of Mexican Tales." In *Puro Mexicano,* edited by J. Frank Dobie. Austin: Texas Folklore Society, 1935.

Ashliman, D. L. *A Guide to Folktales in the English Language, Based on the Aarne-Thompson Classification System.* Westport, Conn.: Greenwood Press, 1987.

Baughman, Ernest W. *Type and Motif Index of the Folktales of England and North America.* The Hague, Netherlands: Mouton and Co., 1966. Indiana University Folklore Series, no. 20.

Bierhorst, John. *Latin American Folktales: Stories from Hispanic and Indian Traditions.* New York: Pantheon Books, 2002.

Boas, Franz. "Notes on Mexican Folklore." *Journal of American Folklore,* vol. 25, 1912.

Boggs, Ralph Steele. *Index of Spanish Folktales.* Chicago: The University of Chicago, Department of Romance Languages and Literatures, 1930. Reprinted from Folklore Fellows Communications no. 90, 1930.

Chase, Richard. *Grandfather Tales.* Boston: Houghton Mifflin, 1948.

Dorson, Richard M. *Buying the Wind: Regional Folklore in the United States.* Chicago and London: University of Chicago Press, 1964.

Espinosa, Aurelio M. *Cuentos Populares Españoles.* Three volumes. Madrid: Consejo Superior de Investigaciones Científicas, 1946–7.

———. "Comparative Notes on New-Mexican and Mexican Spanish Folktales." *Journal of American Folklore,* vol. 27, 1914.

———. *The Folklore of Spain in the American Southwest: Traditional Spanish Folk Literature in Northern New Mexico and Southern Colorado.* Edited by J. Manuel Espinosa. Norman and London: University of Oklahoma Press, 1985.

———. "New-Mexican Spanish Folklore. III: Folktales." *Journal of American Folklore,* vol. 24, 1911.

———. "New-Mexican Spanish Folklore. VII: More Folktales." *Journal of American Folklore,* vol. 27, 1914.

BIBLIOGRAPHY

Espinosa, José Manuel. *Spanish Folktales from New Mexico.* New York: G. E. Stechert, 1937. Memoirs of the American Folklore Society, vol. 30.

———. *Cuentos de Cuanto Hay: Tales from Spanish New Mexico.* Edited and translated by Joe Hayes. Albuquerque: University of New Mexico Press, 1998.

Foster, George M. "Sierra Popoluca Folklore and Beliefs." *University of California Publications in American Archaeology and Ethnology,* no. 42, 1945.

Gatschet, Albert S. "Popular Rimes from Mexico." *Journal of American Folklore,* vol. 2, 1889.

Glazer, Mark. *Flour from Another Sack and Other Proverbs, Folk Beliefs, Tales, Riddles, and Recipes.* Edinburg, Tex.: Pan American University, 1982.

Graham, Joe S. "Mexican Americans." In *American Folklore: An Encyclopedia.* Edited by Jan Harold Brunvand. New York and London: Garland Publishing, 1996.

Griego y Maestas, José, and Rudolfo A. Anaya. *Cuentos: Tales from the Hispanic Southwest.* Santa Fe: Museum of New Mexico Press, 1980.

Hansen, Terrence Leslie. *The Types of the Folktale in Cuba, Puerto Rico, the Dominican Republic, and Spanish South America.* Berkeley, Los Angeles, and London: University of California Press, 1957. Folklore Studies, no. 8.

Hayes, Joe. *The Day It Snowed Tortillas: Tales from Spanish New Mexico.* Santa Fe: Mariposa Publishing, 1982.

———. *Everyone Knows Gato Pinto: More Tales from Spanish New Mexico.* Santa Fe: Mariposa Publishing, 1992.

———. See J. M. Espinosa, *Cuentos de Cuanto Hay.*

Lang, Andrew. *The Orange Fairy Book.* London and New York: Longman, 1906.

Laughlin, Robert M. *Of Cabbages and Kings: Tales from Zinacantán.* Washington: Smithsonian Institution Press, 1977. Smithsonian Contributions to Anthropology, no. 23.

Lea, Aurora Lucero-White. *Literary Folklore of the Hispanic Southwest.* San Antonio, Tex: The Naylor Company, 1953.

Mason, J. Alden. "Folktales of the Tepecanos." *Journal of American Folklore,* vol. 27, 1914.

———. "Four Mexican-Spanish Fairytales from Azqueltán, Jalisco." *Journal of American Folklore,* vol. 25, 1912.

Mechling, Wm. H. "Stories from Tuxtepec, Oaxaca." *Journal of American Folklore,* vol. 25, 1912.

Mendoza, Vicente T., and Virginia Rodríguez Rivera de Mendoza. *Folklore de San Pedro Piedra Gorda, Zacatecas.* Mexico: Instituto Nacional de Bellas Artes, Secretaría de Educación Pública, 1952.

Miller, Elaine K. *Mexican Folk Narrative from the Los Angeles Area.* Austin and London: University of Texas Press. Memoirs of the American Folklore Society, vol. 56.

Paredes, Américo. *Folktales of Mexico.* Chicago and London: University of Chicago Press, 1970.

Parsons, Elsie Clews. "Folklore from Santa Ana Xalmimilulco, Puebla, Mexico." *Journal of American Folklore,* vol. 45, 1932.

———. "Zapoteca and Spanish Tales of Mitla, Oaxaca." *Journal of American Folklore,* vol. 45, 1932.

BIBLIOGRAPHY

——. *Taos Tales.* New York: J. J. Augustin, 1940. Memoirs of the American Folklore Society, vol. 34.

Radin, Paul, and Aurelio M. Espinosa. *El Folklore de Oaxaca.* New York; G. E. Stechert, 1917.

Rael, Juan B. *Cuentos Españoles de Colorado y de Nuevo Méjico.* Two volumes. Stanford, California: Stanford University Press, 1957.

Randolph, Vance. *The Devil's Pretty Daughter and Other Ozark Folktales.* New York: Columbia University Press, 1955.

Redfield, Margaret Park. "The Folk Literature of a Yucatecan Town." *Contributions to American Archaeology,* vol. 3, 1937.

Reid, John Turner. "Seven Folktales from Mexico." *Journal of American Folklore,* vol. 48, 1935.

Robe, Stanley L. *Amapa Storytellers.* Berkeley, Los Angeles, and London: University of California Press, 1972. Folklore Studies, no. 24.

——. *Hispanic Folktales from New Mexico: Narratives from the R. D. Jameson Collection.* Berkeley, Los Angeles, and London: University of California Press, 1977. Folklore Studies, no. 30.

——. *Index of Mexican Folktales.* Berkeley, Los Angeles, and London: University of California Press, 1973. Folklore Studies, no. 26.

——. *Mexican Tales and Legends from Los Altos.* Berkeley, Los Angeles, and London: University of California Press, 1970. Folklore Studies, no. 20.

——. *Mexican Tales and Legends from Veracruz.* Berkeley, Los Angeles, and London: University of California Press, 1971. Folklore Studies, no. 23.

Taggart, James M. *Enchanted Maidens: Gender Relations in Spanish Folktales of Courtship and Marriage.* Princeton, N.J.: Princeton University Press, 1990.

——. *The Bear and His Sons: Masculinity in Spanish and Mexican Folktales.* Austin: University of Texas Press, 1997.

Tully, Marjorie F., and Juan B. Rael. *An Annotated Bibliography of Spanish Folklore in New Mexico and Southern Colorado.* Albuquerque: University of New Mexico Press, 1950. University of New Mexico Publications in Language and Literature, no. 3.

Van Etten, Teresa Pijoan de. *Spanish-American Folktales.* Little Rock, Ark.: August House Publishers, Inc., 1990.

Weigle, Marta. *Two Guadalupes: Hispanic Legends and Magic Tales from Northern New Mexico.* Santa Fe: Ancient City Press, 1987.

West, John O. *Mexican-American Folklore.* Little Rock, Ark.: August House Publishers, 1988.

Wheeler, Howard T. *Tales from Jalisco, Mexico.* Philadelphia: American Folklore Society, 1943. Memoirs of the American Folklore Society, vol. 35.

Yeats, W. B. *Fairy Tales of Ireland.* Edited by Neil Philip. New York: Delacorte Press, 1990.

Zunser, Helen. "A New Mexican Village." *Journal of American Folklore,* vol. 48, 1935.